Written by
Killian Wolf

Published in association with Bear With Us Productions

Paparback ISBN: 978-1-951140-29-8
Hardback ISBN: 978-1-951140-28-1

Cover by Richie Evans
Design by Luisa Moschetti
Illustrated by Alice Pieroni
Edited by: Naomi Shulman

killianwolf.com
www.justbearwithus.com

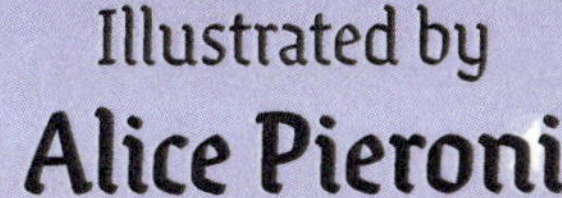

Illustrated by
Alice Pieroni

Written by
Killian Wolf

Klaus trotted through the woods, his basket on his back,
Each step he took left hoofprints deep along the snowy track.
"Dad?" asked Klaus, a little bored, **"Is this all that we do?**
Collecting coal for naughty kids to teach them lessons true?"

"This work is key to Yule," said Dad.

"It's how we make it run.

Without these lumps of coal,

the lessons taught would not get done."

Klaus sighed but kept on trudging forth, his heart still wishing more—
When something strange out in the trees made him forget his chore.

A **shadow** leapt between the pines, a glow within the frost.
"What's that?" asked Klaus, his breath a cloud, his footing nearly lost.
"Stay here," said Dad, his voice quite firm. "We've got too much to do."
But curiosity pulled Klaus; compelled him to pursue.

Through snowy woods, Klaus tracked the
glow, his basket in his hand.
The footprints flickered, fading fast, like
they were drawn in sand.

A **curling fog** began to rise,
and soon the woods were gone.
Instead, a world of strangeness
spread, aglow as if with dawn.

The sights around Klaus made him stop – homes lined with ghostly lights,
While carved-up pumpkins grinned at him with faces full of frights.

And everywhere, **strange children** ran, in capes and masks galore.
They laughed and cheered while bags of treats spilled over on the floor.
"What is this place?" young Klaus inquired, eyes as wide as moons.
The glowing trail ahead now hummed with eerie, lilting tunes.

Then suddenly, the figure stopped and turned to face young Klaus. Its grin was wide, its eyes aglow, its posture full of rouse.

"**Boo!**" it yelled, and Klaus fell back, his basket hitting ground.

The ghoul then cackled, loud and clear — a deep, resounding sound.
"Who are you?" young Klaus exclaimed, his tail swished behind.
The ghoul just smirked and tipped its hat, its grin still unconfined.
"Tatterbone's the name," it said, its voice both rough and sly.
"And you've been brave to follow me — most wouldn't even try!"

"Well, Tatterbones," said Klaus, annoyed, "I think you've gone too far.
You've wandered where you don't belong, from wherever you are!"
"Don't fret, young fella," Tatterbones said with a playful leer.
"I'll show you something magical that only happens here!"

But sooner than Klaus could reply, the ghoul let out a **shout**.
It **dashed** away, its shadow trailing long and winding out.
Klaus gripped his basket, gave a huff. "Oh no, you won't escape!"
And off he ran to chase the ghoul, through fog and misty drape.

The chase went through the glowing streets,
past children dressed in guise.

Klaus **zigged** and **zagged** through spooky yards,
beneath the pumpkin skies.

But suddenly, the ghoul turned back,
its glowing eyes alight.
"It's my turn now!"
it laughed aloud, instilling Klaus with fright.
The tables turned; the ghoul gave chase,
and Klaus began to flee.

"Wait, stop!" Klaus yelled,
though deep inside, he giggled joyfully.
They raced through yards, past candy trails,
skeletons, and bats,
Through bouncing webs and wobbling ghosts
and witches wearing hats.

At last, the ghoul came to a halt, its grin both kind and sly.
It offered Klaus a candy treat and said, "No need to cry.
This holiday's called Halloween. It's not so bad, you see!
We dress up, scare, and trick-or-treat—it's really fun and free!"

Klaus chewed the candy, eyes now wide. "This is... amazing stuff!
I thought you'd ruin Yule, but now, I think I've learned enough."
Tatterbones flashed Klaus a grin. "Fun doesn't have to spoil.
Now let me show you more delights before you end your toil."

For hours more, the two explored the wonders all around,
Until a **voice** rang through the air, a deep and rumbling sound.

"Klaus!" it called, and Klaus went stiff, his fur now bristling tight.

"**Dad?**" he whispered, turning back to see his father's might.
Father Krampus strode through fog, his eyes both sharp and stern.
"Klaus, explain yourself at once. Where did you stray and turn?"

"I... thought the ghoul might ruin Yule," Klaus said, his voice quite small.
"But Dad, he didn't wreck a thing. In fact, I had a ball!"
Tatterbones stepped forward, bowing low, his grin now shy.

"Apologies, sir Krampus, but I have to clarify:
This holiday we celebrate—it's called All Hallow's Eve.
A night of fun and frights, but not a single soul deceives."

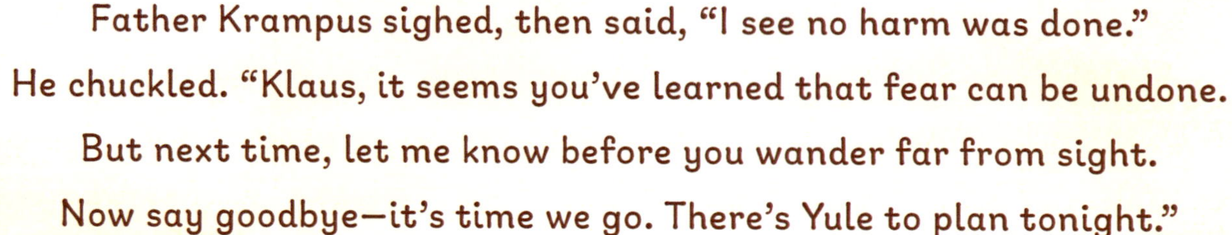

Father Krampus sighed, then said, "I see no harm was done."
He chuckled. "Klaus, it seems you've learned that fear can be undone.
But next time, let me know before you wander far from sight.
Now say goodbye—it's time we go. There's Yule to plan tonight."

Klaus turned back toward Tatterbones, a smile upon his face.
"Thank you for the fun," he said, "and showing me this place."

As Klaus returned to snowy lands, he brought a souvenir—
He held a glowing pumpkin high, a keepsake of his cheer.

The Company

Bear With Us Productions is a company dedicated to illustrating and developing high-quality children's books for new and existing authors all over the world. The company is known for its friendly attitude and professional work ethic which has made them the 'go-to guys,' for high-quality children's book development, predominantly within the self-publishing sector.

Bear With Us Productions employs over 60 children's book illustrators and professional designers from a multitude of places around the world and loves dealing with the rich diversity in illustration styles that this brings to the numerous projects the company develops.

justbearwithus.com
FB: @bearwithusproductions
IG: bear_with_us_productions

The Illustrator

Alice Pieroni was born in Fano, Italy in 1991.
She graduated with a degree in illustration from the "International School of Comics," and started illustrating children's books because she has always wanted to make children happy through her drawings.
Her style is constantly evolving, and every day she strives to improve herself, preferring colours that recall traditional ones, such as watercolours and pencils.

She collaborated with Bear With Us Production for the books "Little Krampus and the Magical Sleigh Ride," "Santa Goes Sledding on Christmas Eve," and "Little Krampus and the Christmas Secret."
She also worked with some publishing houses in recent years including Dami Editori, Editions Grenouille, Auggie Bear Publishing, Little Lamb Books, and Gribaudo Edizioni.

www.ingramcontent.com/pod-product-compliance
Lightning Source LLC
Chambersburg PA
CBRC092147180726
48295CB00008B/130